by Sarah Hines Stephens

POOCHES OF POWER!

illustrated by
Art Baltazar

Batman created by Bob Kane

Superman created by
Jerry Siegel and Joe Shuster

Picture Window Books™
a capstone imprint

Starring...

ACE
THE BAT-HOUND!

KRYPTO
THE SUPER-DOG!

THE BAD NEWS BIRDS!

BATMAN!

WADDLES!

ARTIE PUFFIN!

GRIFF!

THE PENGUIN!

TABLE OF CONTENTS!

BATCAVE
BAT-COMPUTER

SUPER-PET HERO FILE 005:

ACE

Ultra-hearing

Bat-cowl

Ultra-smell

Utility Collar

Fireproof Cape

Bat-symbol

Powerful Paws

Super Hero Owner:
BATMAN

Species: Bat-Hound

Place of Birth: Gotham City

Age: Unknown

Favorite Food:
Crime Fighter Crunchies

Bio: Batman found Ace while solving a case. Unable to find the owner, the Dark Knight kept the dog and nicknamed him "The Bat-Hound." Ace considers himself Batman's partner, *not* his pet.

Chapter 1

WHIFF OF TROUBLE

Ace the Bat-Hound stretched his legs. He settled at billionaire Bruce Wayne's feet. The two crime fighters were back from their nightly rounds and enjoying their morning. While their butler, Alfred, served tea, Bruce and Ace relaxed with the paper.

This morning, the news was
not helping Ace relax. There was
something fishy about the headline.
"Missing Fish at Sardine Factory,"
Bruce read aloud. **GRRRR!**
Those words made

the fur on Ace's neck

stand up.

MISSING FISH
AT SARDINE FACTORY

Ace knew the factory well. It was located on the Gotham City docks — a favorite hangout for thieves and thugs.

Batman and Ace often patrolled the area. Whenever they passed the factory, the workers would toss Ace a sardine treat.

Lately, however, the workers didn't have a fish to spare. According to the paper, they didn't even have enough to fill their cans. The fishermen were catching as much as always, but the factory was coming up short.

Somebody must be stealing the fish between the fishing boats and the factory, Ace thought. *But who? And how?* The questions bothered Ace like an itchy flea under his Utility Collar.

The moment Bruce left for work, Ace streaked through his dog door. He headed toward the Gotham City docks.

When he arrived, everything looked and smelled normal. Still, something didn't feel right.

Most of the fishing boats were out at sea. The crowd of shady people that hung around at night had turned in. The factory workers hadn't yet arrived for the morning shift. It was so quiet. **_Too quiet,_** the Bat-Hound thought.

As he moved closer to the factory, Ace slowed down. With his canine hearing, he sensed someone coming.

BEEP! BEEP! BEEP!

Suddenly, a gadget on Ace's Utility Collar sounded an alarm. It had picked up someone, or something, in the shadows by the back doors of the factory.

FWOOSH!

"**Krypto!**" Ace greeted his friend the Super-Dog. "I thought I might find you here."

With his super-sniffing powers,
Krypto had smelled trouble on the
docks long before anyone else. He had
already been nosing around for clues
and found something.

SNIFF! SNIFF!

"I sniffed out some evidence," the
Super-Dog barked. **"Follow me!"**

Krypto soared to the rooftop of a
warehouse connected to the factory.

WOOOOSH!

"Up here," he said. "Need a lift?"

Ace didn't bother to answer. The
Bat-Hound couldn't fly. He had his
own way of getting around. Taking
huge leaps, he made his way up. He
jumped from a pile of crates, to a
cargo bin, and onto the roof.

Once there, Ace only needed a

second to understand the clue Krypto

had found. The feathers lying on the

rooftop could mean only one thing . . .

"The Bad News Birds," Ace growled.

FOWL PLAY

The feathers Krypto had found were a sure sign of **Batman's evil enemy the Penguin!** His sidekicks must have been spending time on the docks.

The blue feather belonged to **Waddles,** the evil penguin. The white-tipped vulture feather was **Griff's.**

The black feathers had to be **Artie the puffin's.** Together, the three birds were a flock of trouble.

"Does this mean Penguin is behind the missing fish?" Krypto asked.

Ace's eyes narrowed. The criminal was behind a lot of Gotham's crime. Ace wanted to pin the blame for the missing fish on him, too. But he didn't have enough proof. Besides, Ace didn't think Penguin could make enough money stealing sardines to feed his greedy appetite.

The Bat-Hound needed more information before he could point a paw at Penguin. Luckily, he and Krypto had a bird's-eye view of the docks. As they checked the area, the Dog Duo heard squawks from inside.

SQUAWK! SQUAWK!

Ace and Krypto looked through a skylight into the warehouse below. Through the glass, they saw a black and white creature. It wore a top hat and was enjoying a slice of pizza. **It was the Penguin!**

"There he is!" Krypto growled.

"Let's get him." The Super-Dog was ready to break the glass. He wanted to catch the villain while he ate.

"Hold on," said the Bat-Hound. **"We need proof first."**

"Isn't that proof enough?" Krypto asked, pointing below. Penguin's pizza was piled high with sardines — the same fish missing from the factory.

"One giant pizza doesn't explain thousands of missing fish," said Ace.

Ace's eyes locked on a wobbling bird delivering Penguin's lunch. **Waddles!** "But maybe *he* can help," growled the Bat-Hound.

Ace watched Waddles walk toward his boss with another sardine pizza. Penguin gave it a sniff. Then he sent the pizza sailing across the room.

SQUAWK! SQUAWK!

"I'm sick of pizza," Penguin said. He waved his deadly umbrella. "And I am sick of hiding. When are we going to be ready?!"

Ace put his head closer to the glass.
He knew who Penguin was hiding
from. He was hiding from Batman.
The super hero had gathered enough
evidence from other crimes to lock
Penguin up for good.

"Take it easy, boss," Waddles said.

He scooped the fish off the floor. "It's

not so bad here."

"Not so bad?!" Penguin screeched.

"Beats prison," Waddles replied.

The Penguin tapped his umbrella on

the floor angrily. Waddles had a point.

Rotting in jail would be worse.

"We just need to lay low a little

longer," Waddles added, backing out of

the room. **"We're almost ready to go."**

"**Ready to go where?**" Ace asked himself.

BEEP!

The Bat-Hound pushed a button on his collar. He sent an electronic message to the **Batcave.** He had recorded everything he'd just seen. The video would alert Batman to the Penguin's location.

"**Can we get him now?**" Krypto asked.

"**Soon,**" Ace said in a low growl. "Two slices of pizza are only part of the pie. We still need more proof."

The Bat-Hound hoped to get to the bottom of this factory caper. As he spoke, Ace watched Waddles walk toward the door.

"**Follow that bird!**" he directed the Super-Dog. "Waddles might lead us to the next clue."

FWOOOSH!

Krypto flew from the rooftop after the evil bird.

While the Super-Dog kept on eye on Waddles, Ace investigated. On the top of the factory, the Bat-Hound spotted a fish-sorting machine. An attached funnel was where fishermen unloaded their catch of the day.

Ace looked inside. Though the day was warming up, a cool breeze blew out of the machine and across Ace's nose. Just like that, he knew exactly where the rest of the Bad News Birds were cooling their heels.

Ace leaped down from the roof the way he'd come up. He needed a way inside the factory. The second story window would work just fine.

Ace pushed a button on his collar. He launched a **Batarang** and wire.

FWOOOOOSH!!

CLANK! The Batarang

caught on the edge of the roof. Ace

pulled himself up the wire and inside.

The factory was dark. Ace slipped

through the shadows. He stopped in

front of a locked freezer door.

"Waddles is inside the freezer," Krypto said, walking up beside Ace.

"And the other birds?" Ace asked.

Krypto took a look with his **X-ray vision.** "Griff and Artie are in there, too," he said.

The three birds were resting beside what looked like a long slide. They had been using the funnel to steal the sardines!

"We've got to get in there," Ace growled. **"Now!"**

IN THE CAN

Krypto focused his **heat vision** on the steel door. Laser beams blasted out of his eyes. They melted the door's hinges. *TSSSSSSS!*

The door hit the ground. **CLANG!** The birds looked up to see Ace and Krypto blocking any chance of escape.

"Help!" shouted Waddles, rolling onto his feet.

Artie blinked, gripping fish in his beak. Griff shivered in silence.

"The gig is up, sardine snatchers," Ace growled. "We've only got one choice to make. Should we hand you over to the police now? Or should we let your boss punish you first?"

"Punish us for what?" Artie asked.

"Foiling his escape plan," Ace said.

BLEEP! Suddenly, a whistle blew outside the factory. Artie smiled. Before the Dog Duo knew what was happening, ten tons of fish came sliding down the funnel.

SPLOOSH!

The fishy flood picked up the birds and dogs. It carried them out the freezer door and onto the factory floor.

Artie was the first one back on his feet. The puffin took out his pair of **ice dice**. He gave them a roll.

Ace showed his teeth. No matter what numbers Artie rolled, the results would be ugly. When the dice stopped, two dots stared up from the cubes. The high-tech weapon froze Krypto and Ace in their tracks.

"So long, you mangy mutts!" Artie called out.

Griff pulled Waddles to his feet. They sprinted out of the factory. Artie grabbed his dice and flapped after them. They were getting away!

"We have to stop them!" Ace barked. He could barely move his frozen snout.

Once again, Krypto came to the rescue. Using his heat vision, he quickly thawed himself and Ace.

BZZZZZT!!

"You go that way," Ace said.

Krypto took off like a shot. Ace paused for a moment. The Bat-Hound had spotted an escape hatch.

Lifting the door to the hatch with his teeth, Ace dropped into a tube. He slid into the fishy darkness.

After a moment, Ace splashed to a stop in a large room filled with tanks. He had fallen so far down, he thought he must be underground.

Then suddenly, the Bat-Hound knew that he was underwater. **He was inside Penguin's secret submarine!**

All around him, the Dog Detective saw large barrels of fish oil. The barrels were connected by tubes to the sub's high-tech fuel tanks. By turning sardines into oil, Penguin planned to power his sub and escape Gotham.

"Not if I can help it," Ace growled.

The Bat-Hound quickly exited the

sub through a small hatch. Using his

special air hose, Ace swam underwater.

He headed back to the docks to stop

Penguin's plan.

Still wet with ocean water, Ace entered the factory. He spotted the bad birds hiding in the rafters.

"Thought you'd fly the coop, did you?" he barked.

Ace pulled a tiny grenade from his collar. He removed the pin and kicked the explosive away with his back legs.

KA-BLAMO!

The noise startled everyone in the factory. No one was hurt, but it gave Ace the chance he needed.

The Bat-Hound set his flashlight on a table. He turned it on. Then he launched a Batarang at the light switch. **FWIP!** The room went dark, except for the single spotlight.

Using his paws, Ace created a shadow in the shape of Penguin on the wall. Then he pushed a button on his Utility Collar. He played back the voice recording he had made earlier.

"You're done for!" the Penguin's voice boomed through the room.

"**Ah!**" screamed Waddles, Artie, and Griff. The Bad News Birds ran in all directions. They tripped over each other with fright. **SQUAWK!**

Ace's plan worked perfectly. Without waiting, he tossed his Batarang. He tied the birds together. Then he swung them onto a nearby machine.

"**Nice work,**" said a deep voice behind Ace. It was **Batman.** He stepped into the factory, holding onto the Penguin. "Looks like we're both out bird hunting today."

The Penguin growled. He struggled to get away. The villain didn't stand a chance. **"How'd you find me anyway, Batty?"** Penguin asked.

"Let's just say a little bird told me," Batman replied.

Penguin spotted his wingmen tied up on the cleaning and canning machine. He struggled harder. "I would have been long gone if you lousy fish-eaters hadn't been eating all of my fuel!" Penguin shouted.

Griff, Waddles, and Artie were swept into the sardine machine. The criminal turned his glare on Ace. **"Is this mutt yours?"** he asked Batman.

"No," Batman replied. **"We just run in the same pack."**

Ace held his head high. But this was no time to celebrate. The job was not wrapped up yet. He was beginning to worry about Krypto. He hadn't seen his friend since they had escaped from the freezer. The Super-Dog never missed out on the action.

"We'll never fit," Artie moaned as the birds came out from the cleaner, their feathers plucked. The next stop on the belt was where fish were pressed into tiny cans.

"Not to worry," said a voice outside.

Krypto was back, and he had a surprise! The Super-Dog flew in fast. He was carrying a sardine can large enough to fit the flock. He scooped up the birds and stuck them inside.

"Don't you know, stealing is foul play?" Krypto asked, wagging his tail.

"That's right," Ace agreed. "We're putting you dirty birds right where you belong."

"In the can!" they both barked.

END!

KNOW YOUR

Krypto

Streaky

Beppo

Comet

Ace

Jumpa

Whatzit

B'dg

Storm

Topo

Ark

Hoppy

Paw Pooch

Bull Dog

Chameleon Collie

Hot Dog

Aw yeah, **HERO PETS!**

Tail Terrier

Tusky Husky

SUPER-PETS!

Ignatius

Chauncey

Crackers

Giggles

Artie Puffin

Griff

Waddles

Rozz

Dex-Starr

Glomulus

Misty

Sneezers

Whoosh

Pronto

Snorrt

Rolf

Squealer

Kajunn

Aw yeah, **VILLAIN PETS!**

AW YEAH, JOKES!

Hey, Krypto! What kind of dog has the most ticks?

What?!

A watch dog!

Why are Dalmatians no good at "Hide and Seek"?

Beats me.

They're always spotted!

It's raining cats and dogs outside.

How do you know?

I just stepped in a poodle!

WORD POWER!

Batarang (BAT-uh-rayng)—a high-tech weapon used by the Bat-Hound

evidence (EV-uh-duhnss)—information or facts that help prove something or make you believe that something is true

patrolled (puh-TROHLD)—walked around an area to protect it or keep watch on people

sardine (sar-DEEN)—a small saltwater fish, often sold in a can as food

sidekick (SIDE-kik)—a partner, or a person who works for and helps out another person

Utility Collar (yoo-TIL-uh-tee KOL-ur)—a thin band worn around the Bat-Hound's neck, which contains all of his secret gadgets

MEET THE AUTHOR!

Sarah Hines Stephens

Sarah Hines Stephens has authored more than 60 books for children and written about all kinds of characters, from Jedi to princesses. When she is not writing, gardening, or saving the world by teaching about recycling, Sarah enjoys spending time with her heroic husband, two kids, and super friends.

MEET THE ILLUSTRATOR!

Eisner Award-winner Art Baltazar

Art Baltazar is a cartoonist machine from the heart of Chicago! He defines cartoons and comics not only as an art style, but as a way of life. Currently, Art is the creative force behind *The New York Times* best-selling, Eisner Award-winning, DC Comics series Tiny Titans and the co-writer for *Billy Batson and the Magic of SHAZAM!* Art is living the dream! He draws comics and never has to leave the house. He lives with his lovely wife, Rose, big boy Sonny, little boy Gordon, and little girl Audrey. Right on!

Art Baltazar says:

Read all of the DC SUPER-PETS stories today!

▦ Picture Window Books™

Published in 2011
A Capstone Imprint
151 Good Counsel Drive, P.O. Box 669
Mankato, Minnesota 56002
www.capstonepub.com

Cataloging-in-Publication Data is available at the
Library of Congress website.

ISBN: 978-1-4048-6306-4 (library binding)
ISBN: 978-1-4048-6620-1 (paperback)

Summary: Ace the Bat-Hound and Krypto
the Super-Dog smell something fishy.
Penguin's Bad News Birds have stolen
sardines from the Gotham City Marina.
Together, the doggy duo must reel in the
fowl felons and throw them in the can!

Art Director & Designer: Bob Lentz
Editor: Donald Lemke
Production Specialist: Michelle Biedscheid
Creative Director: Heather Kindseth
Editorial Director: Michael Dahl
Publisher: Lori Benton

Printed in the United States of America
in Stevens Point, Wisconsin.
092010   005934WZS11